Scientist's Word List

SCIENTIST – A person who tries to make discoveries about how the world works

SCIENTIFIC INSTINCT – A natural impulse to use scientific ideas to think about a problem

HYPOTHESIS – An idea or a guess about the answer to a problem before a person tests it

CALCULATION – A way to solve a scientific or mathematical problem, often using numbers

EXPERIMENT – A test that gives information to help solve a problem

OBSERVE – To watch and listen carefully

RESULT – The information a person learns from an experiment

PiRATE, ViKiNG & SCiENTiST

JARED CHAPMAN

L B

LITTLE, BROWN AND COMPANY

New York   Boston

Pirate was friends with Scientist.

Scientist was friends with Viking.

Viking and Pirate were not friends...

...not even on Scientist's birthday.

Pirate gave Scientist his gift.
Then Viking showed up.

So Pirate welcomed
him to the party.

...until his scientific
instinct kicked in.

What could smooth things over between his friends?
Scientist had a hypothesis.
Maybe BIRTHDAY CAKE was the answer.

Viking offered to cut the cake, but Pirate decided to help himself.

Viking suggested he wait.

Viking was boiling. Pirate was bloated.
Scientist was irritated (and covered in cake).

Scientist studied his results. He didn't get the outcome he'd wanted, but he wasn't giving up.

Maybe PARTY GAMES could help turn these foes into friends!

The two fell to the floor in a brawling heap!

Scientist was stumped.
Why weren't his experiments working?
Were his calculations off?

Pirate blamed Viking. Viking blamed Pirate. Scientist cut them off. "I'm trying to think!"

Scientist's friends were so much alike.
Why did they have to keep fighting?
Scientist thought about what
made Pirate and Viking happy.
He scribbled and scrawled.
He marked and measured.

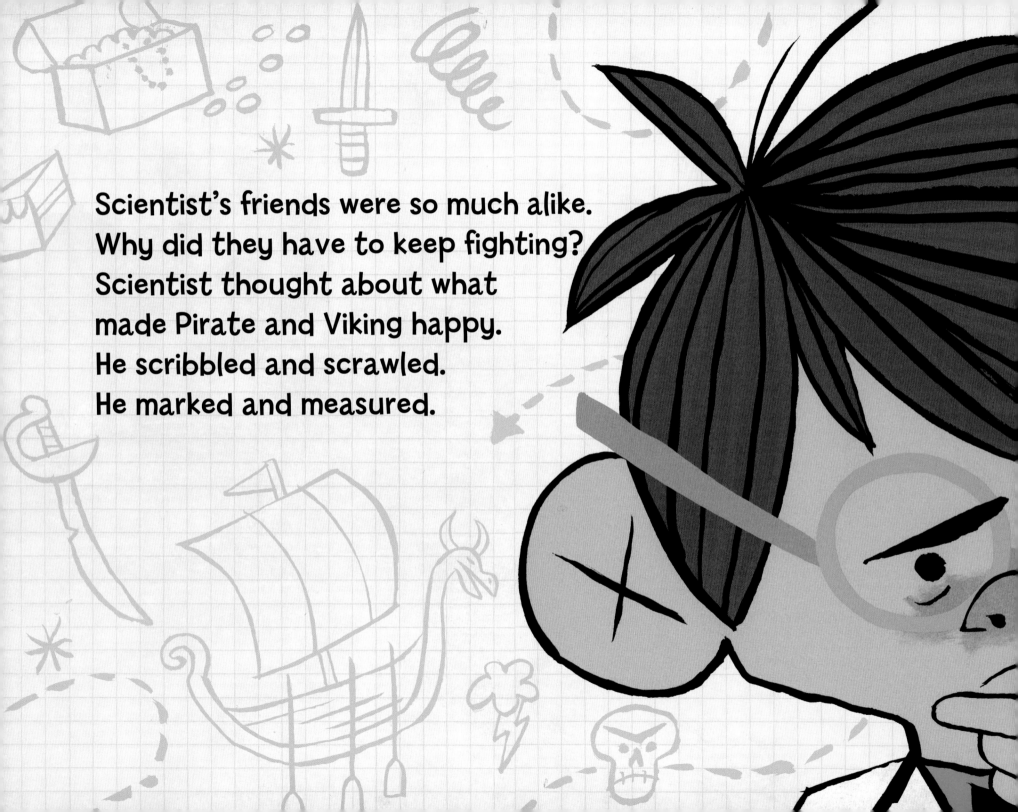

And he decided to try one final experiment.

"Do you like boats?"
Scientist asked his friends.
Pirate and Viking nodded...
in between punches.

"And what do you keep under your pillows at night?" Scientist asked.

Pirate and Viking stopped fighting and looked at Scientist. "A sword," they answered.

Now Scientist asked
his last question:
"What's your favorite way
to spend Saturday mornings?"

PILLAGING AND

Pirate and Viking burst into laughter.
Scientist observed proudly.
His experiment was
finally a success!

Pirate was friends with Scientist.
Scientist was friends with Viking.
And now Pirate and Viking
were friends.

The three pals decided it
was time for ice cream...

...and a little pillaging and plundering.

For my mom and dad

• Little, Brown and Company • Hachette Book Group • 237 Park Avenue, New York, NY 10017 • Visit our website at lb-kids.com • Little, Brown and Company is a division of Hachette Book Group, Inc. • The Little, Brown name and logo are trademarks of Hachette Book Group, Inc. • The publisher is not responsible for websites (or their content) that are not owned by the publisher. • First Edition: November 2014 • Library of Congress Cataloging-in-Publication Data • Chapman, Jared, author, illustrator. • Pirate, Viking & Scientist / Jared Chapman. • pages cm • Summary: "A pirate and a Viking fight to become the very best friend of a kid scientist, who meanwhile devises the perfect formula for all three friends to play happily together"—Provided by publisher. • ISBN 978-0-316-25389-5 (hardcover) • [1. Friendship—Fiction. 2. Experiments—Fiction.] I. Title. II. Title: Pirate, Viking and Scientist. • PZ7.C3678Pi 2014 • [E]—dc23 • 2013022289 • 10 9 8 7 6 5 4 3 2 1 • SC • Printed in China

About This Book

The illustrations in this book were drawn with ink from
Pirate's pet octopus and an old, ratty brush that Viking
found at the bottom of the ocean. For the digital coloring,
Scientist created a supercomputer that is already
hard at work on a new story.

This book was edited by Andrea Spooner and Deirdre Jones
and designed by Phil Caminiti with art direction by
Patti Ann Harris. The production was supervised by
Erika Schwartz, and the production editor was Christine Ma.

This book was printed on 128-gsm Gold Sun matte paper. The
text was set in Billy, and the display type was hand-lettered.